ERNIE the ERASER

Ashlyn Parker

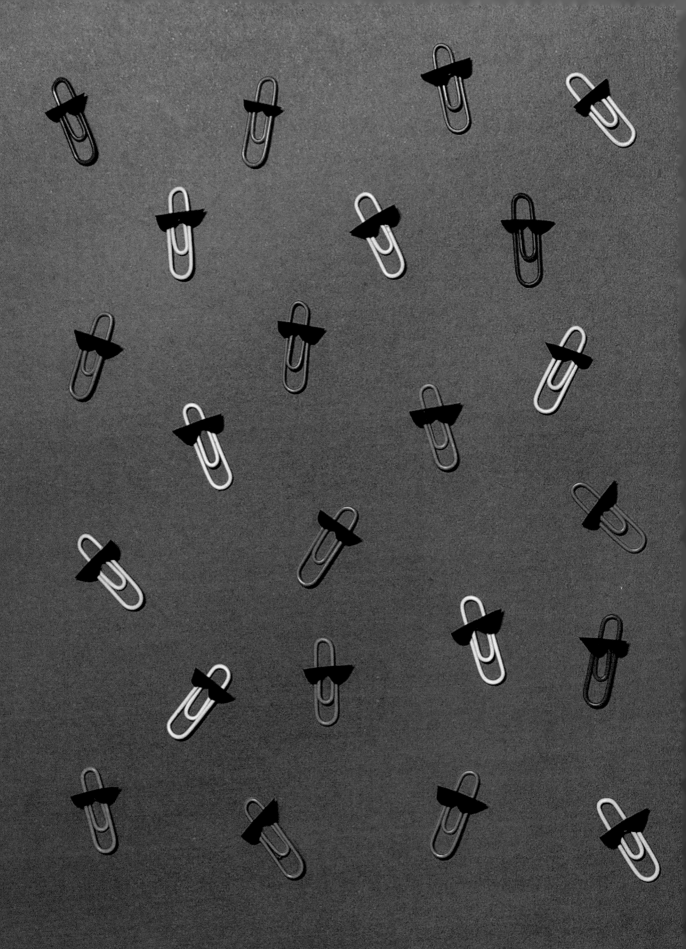

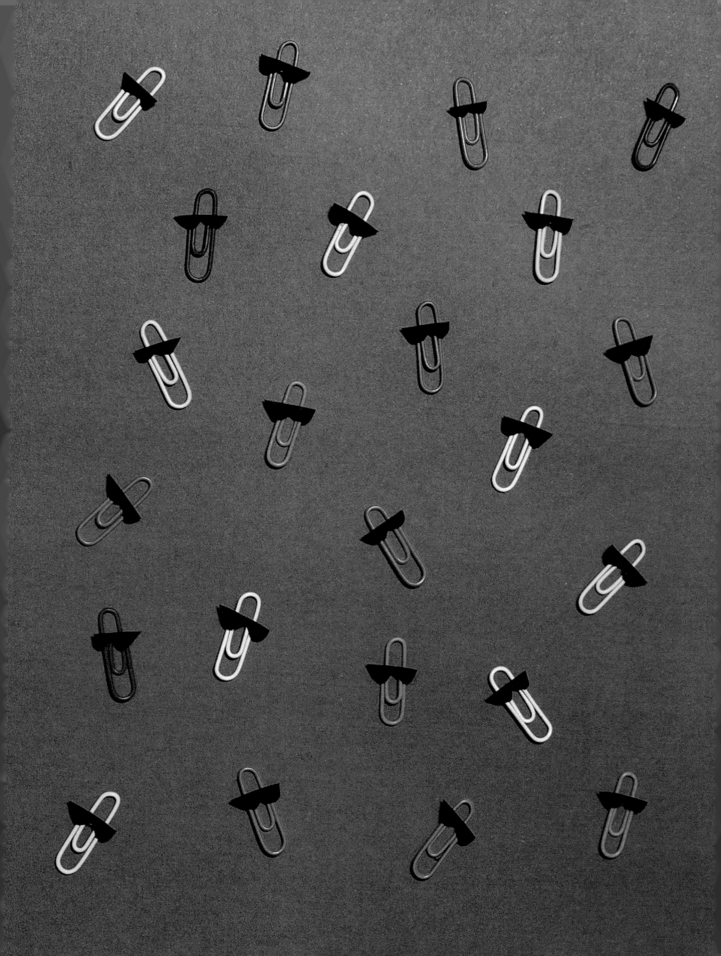

Made in the USA
Middletown, DE
15 August 2019

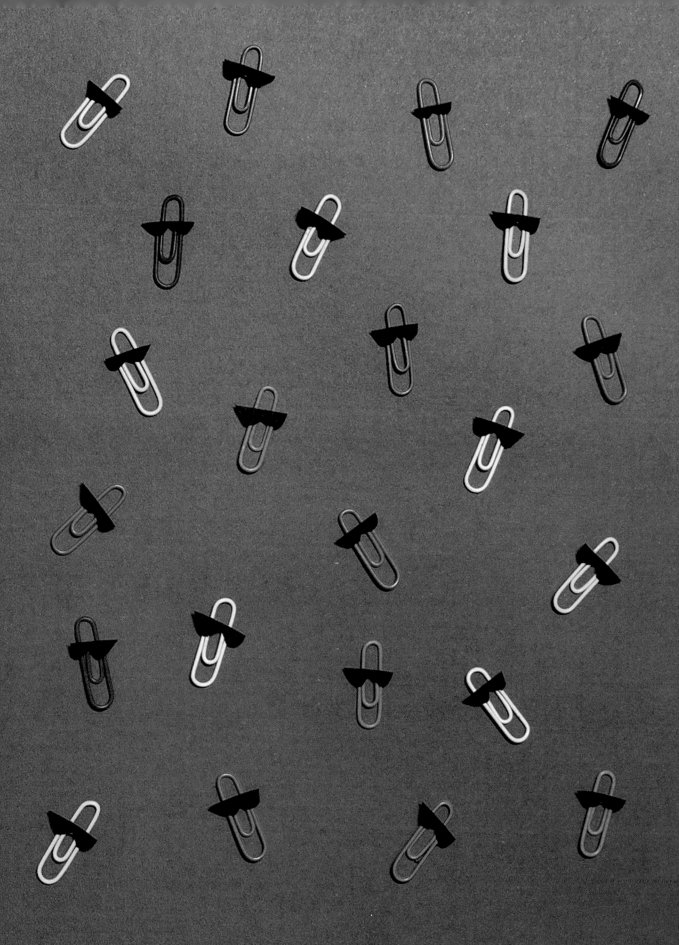

To Patsy and Ernie
for their constant love and support.

To Mom and Dad
for their dedication to teaching.

FIRST EDITION

ISBN 978-1-7330407-0-9 (paperback)

www.bethelightlivebright.com

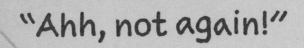

"Ahh, not again!"

Ernie the Eraser braces himself.

He knows the sounds
mistakes make.
It's his job to clean them up.

His student, Jen, lifts Patsy the Pencil from her cat drawing.

"Cats don't have circles for noses, they have triangles!" Jen says.

Patsy frowns.
Ernie can tell she thinks
it's all her fault.

"It's okay, Patsy!" he says.

Patsy squints and looks away.

Ernie's cheeks turn even more pink.
He always gets dirty looks from the pencils
since he only shows up at bad times.

They don't understand that he doesn't
rub *in* their mistakes...

he works hard to rub them *away!*

Jen picks up Ernie.

As she presses him to the nose,
he begins to sing his mess-up song:

Scrub and rub, rub and scrub.
Don't worry! I will fix your flub.
Smear and clear, disappear.
Time to try again, my dear!

Ernie made up this song to cheer on the pencils when they make mistakes.

He hopes he will have friends one day if he keeps rooting for them.

Before he can talk to
Patsy again,
Jen slams Ernie
back down on the desk.

Since he is made of rubber,
he bounces high

and flies off the desk.

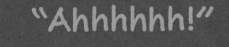

"Ahhhhhh!"

Ernie hits the floor with another huge bounce. He skips and skids to a stop under the teacher's desk.

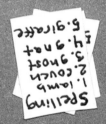

Spelling
1. lamb
2. couch
3. ghost
4. gnat
5. giraffe

MRS. TUBBS

The bell RINGS!

Jen places Patsy and her paper
inside the desk – where *he* should be.

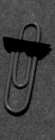

She takes one look
around her desk
for Ernie,
shrugs and leaves.

Ernie panics!

He flips as fast as he can back to his home.

"Eeeek!"

But when he finally gets there,
everyone is gone.

Ernie jumps as high as he can to reach the towering desk.

He is not even close!

He rushes to a nearby trash can. All that's around it is a spoon, a rock, and a pen lid.

"Bingo!" Ernie shouts.

He leans the spoon on the lid, sits on the handle,

and tosses the rock to the other side.

He catapults through the air
faster than a soccer ball at recess.

That is,
until he crashes straight into the desk leg.

Ernie is dazed,

but **not** done.

He returns to the trash
and peels away a wad of chewed gum.

Ernie holds it close to him and leaps at the desk.

He sticks himself to it perfectly,
but when he tries to pull back,
he is stuck.

"Help!" he yells.
But no one answers.

Ernie is not surprised.
After all,
he has no friends.

He sighs.

"I give up."

But then something above Ernie moves.
It's the Paper Clip Pack!

They link together one by one
and make a long chain swing.

With one yank, they free Ernie.

He balances on the swing
as stiff as a ruler while they lift him
to the top.

When he gets there,
he cannot believe what he sees!

It's Patsy the Pencil who holds
the Paper Clip Pack swing.
She smiles down at him.

She pats his back. All the other pencils and school supplies gather around them and chant, "Yay, Ernie! Welcome back!"

Finally, Ernie knows the sounds mistakes AND friends make.

He laughs.

"This is one mess-up
I'll never erase."

The End

About the Author

Ashlyn Parker is a writer who has
shared stories in newspapers,
TV news, blogs and books.
She illustrates with cardstock
and photography.

As a child, she won the Reading Rainbow
Young Writer & Illustrators contest
two years in a row. She told a news reporter,
"When I grow up, I want to be an arthur!"

Twenty years later, she met that goal.